My Weird School #18

Mrs. Yonkers Is Bonkers!

Dan Gutman

Pictures by
Jim Paillot

 HarperTrophy®
An Imprint of HarperCollins Publishers

Mrs. Yonkers Is Bonkers!

Text copyright © 2007 by Dan Gutman

Illustrations copyright © 2007 by Jim Paillot

All rights reserved. Printed in the United States of America.

No part of this book may be used or reproduced in any manner whatsoever without written permission except in the case of brief quotations embodied in critical articles and reviews. For information address HarperCollins Children's Books, a division of HarperCollins Publishers, 195 Broadway, New York, NY 10007.

www.harpercollinschildrens.com

Library of Congress Cataloging-in-Publication Data is available.

ISBN-10: 0-06-123476-1 (lib. bdg.) — ISBN-13: 978-0-06-123476-7 (lib. bdg.)

ISBN-10: 0-06-123475-3 (pbk.) — ISBN-13: 978-0-06-123475-0 (pbk.)

Typography by Joel Tippie

❖

First Harper Trophy edition, 2007

17 18 19 20 OPM 30 29 28 27 26 25

To Emma

Contents

A Computer in My Head

My name is A.J. and I hate school.

Do you know what would be cool? Instead of learning stuff in school, we should have computers built into our heads. There could be software for math, social studies, reading, and all that other stuff teachers say we need to know. You could just plug whatever software you need right into your head. Then we wouldn't have to go to school anymore!*

Think about it. If we had computers in our heads, we could spend more time doing stuff we *want* to do, like playing sports and video games and going to the movies and eating junk food. *That* would be cool. I would buy one of those computers in a minute. But I guess until somebody invents a computer you plug into your head, we'll just have to keep going to school. Bummer in the summer!

We had just finished circle time in Miss

---

*What are you looking down here for? The story is up there, dumbhead.

Daisy's class when Mr. Klutz came into the room. He's the principal of Ella Mentry School, and he has no hair at all. I mean *none*. Hats must slide off his head because there's nothing to hold them on.

"To what do we owe the pleasure of your visit, Mr. Klutz?" asked Miss Daisy. (That's grown-up talk for "What are *you* doing here?")

"I wanted to try out a new joke," Mr. Klutz said.

Oh no! Mr. Klutz tells the worst jokes in the history of the world.**

"Where's the best place to keep a remote

**I can't believe you looked down again!

3

control?" he asked.

"Where?" we all shouted.

"In a remote location!" he said. "Get it? Remote? Location?"

Mr. Klutz bent over laughing and slapped his knee even though his joke

was totally lame. We all laughed anyway. You should always laugh at the principal's jokes, no matter how lame they are. That's the first rule of being a kid.

"But seriously," Mr. Klutz said, putting on his serious face so we knew it was time to get serious, "I need to talk to you about something. Dr. Carbles, the president of the Board of Education, wants us to bring Ella Mentry School into the 21st century."

"Cool!" I shouted. "We're gonna travel through time!"***

"This *is* the 21st century, Arlo," said

***It would be cool to travel through time. If I could travel through time, I'd go to the future when I don't have to go to school anymore.

Andrea Young, this annoying girl with curly brown hair. She calls me by my real name because she knows I hate it.

"I knew that," I said, even though I really didn't. Only a smarty-pants-know-it-all like Andrea would know what number century it is. What is her problem? Who counts centuries?

"How are we going to bring our school into the 21st century, Mr. Klutz?" asked Andrea's crybaby friend Emily, who is allergic to ferrets.

"We're going to spiff up the place," he replied. "We're getting some new equipment, a security guard, a computer lab, and a computer teacher, too. In fact, she's right outside. Would you like to meet Mrs. Yonkers?"

"Yeah!" said all the girls.

"No!" said all the boys.

Mr. Klutz went into the hallway and came back with some lady. You'll never believe in a million hundred years what she had on her head.

I'm not gonna tell you.

Okay, okay, I'll tell you. But you have to read the next chapter. So nah-nah-nah boo-boo on you.

Say Good-bye
to Sugar

Mrs. Yonkers was really weird looking.
She was wearing a polka dot skirt and
one of those big foam fake cheese things
on her head.

"Howdy, y'all!" she said.

She must be from Texas. People from
Texas say "Y'all" and "Yee-ha" all the time

on TV. Nobody knows why.

"In my younger days," Mr. Klutz told us, "I used to work with computers. But Mrs. Yonkers is a computer *expert*. What are the children going to learn in computer class, Mrs. Yonkers?"

"Well," she said, clapping her hands together, "we're going to make our own web-sites, create computer art and computer music, and play virtual reality games. I'll show you some of my own inventions, too. I have so many ideas rumbling around in my head!"

"Doesn't that sound like fun?" asked Mr. Klutz.

"Yeah!" said all the girls.

"No!" said all the boys.

Actually it *did* sound like fun. I just like saying no when grown-ups try to get me to say yes.

"Too bad there isn't a computer program that makes up jokes," Mr. Klutz said. "I could use one of them."

"I'll work on that," said Mrs. Yonkers. "This afternoon I'll be seeing you kids in the new computer lab. But does anybody have any questions before I leave?"

"Why are you wearing a fake piece of cheese on your head?" asked my friend Ryan, who will eat anything, even stuff that isn't food.

"Isn't it funky?" asked Mrs. Yonkers. "I bought it on eBay for twelve cents. Plus ten dollars for shipping. Any other questions?"

"Are you a nerd?" asked my friend Michael, who never ties his shoes.

"That's not very nice, Michael," said Miss Daisy.

But Mrs. Yonkers didn't mind. She pulled up her sweater and showed us a T-shirt she had on underneath. It said NERDS R COOL.

"Say it loud!" she shouted. "I'm a nerd and I'm proud!"

Mrs. Yonkers is weird.

A few minutes later, Mr. Klutz and Mrs. Yonkers left. Guess who walked in the door next? Nobody, because if you walked in a door it would hurt. But guess

who walked in the door*way*?

It was Mrs. Cooney, our school nurse! She has eyes that look like cotton candy, and she is beautiful. She wanted to marry me a while back, but I told her I wouldn't because she's already married to some guy named Mr. Cooney.

"To what do we owe the pleasure of your visit, Mrs. Cooney?" asked Miss Daisy.

"Mr. Klutz asked me to help bring our school into the 21st century," Mrs. Cooney said.

"How are you going to do that?" asked Miss Daisy.

"Well, a big problem these days is that

too many kids are obese," said Mrs. Cooney.

"Too many kids are beasts?" I asked. I was thinking about beasts because I just saw this cool movie called *King Kong*.

"'Obese' is 'fat,' Arlo," said Andrea.

"So is your face," I told her.

Andrea probably looked up "obese" in her dictionary. She keeps one on her desk so she can look up words and show everybody how smart she is. I hate her.

Mrs. Cooney told us that kids need to eat more vegetables and other stuff that doesn't taste good.

"Candy and sweets rot your teeth and dull your mind," said Mrs. Cooney. "Did you know that a can of soda pop contains about *nine* teaspoons of sugar? They call it junk food for a reason."

"What's the reason?" I asked.

"Because it's junk!" she said.

Oh. I thought it was a trick question.

"How are we going to get our students to drink less soda pop and eat less junk food?" asked Miss Daisy.

"I'm glad you asked," said Mrs. Cooney. She held up a poster that said SAY GOOD-BYE TO SUGAR on it. "Starting tomorrow, soda pop and junk food will no longer be allowed inside Ella Mentry School."

WHAT??????????????????????????????

Did I hear that right? No more soda

pop? No more candy?

Suddenly everybody was talking and whispering to one another.

"They've gotta be kidding!" said Michael. "I'll *die* without junk food."

"Life will be horrible," said Neil, who we call Neil the nude kid even though he wears clothes.

"This is gonna be worse than National Poetry Month!" said Ryan.

"This is gonna be worse than TV Turnoff Week!" I said.

"You boys are silly," said Andrea. "I think 'Say Good-bye to Sugar' is a great idea. I *like* healthy food. My favorite foods are herb-roasted chicken, fresh fruit, and baked soy chips."****

"Could you possibly be any more boring?" I asked her.

"You'll feel a lot better once you start eating less junk food," Mrs. Cooney told us.

****Herb-roasted chicken is chicken that is roasted by a guy named Herb.

"How about we give up vegetables instead?" I suggested.

"Arlo, you probably never even *tasted* a vegetable," said Andrea.

"I did too," I told her. "I tasted one once. Then I spit it out."

My friend Billy who lives around the corner told me that if you eat too many vegetables, you get a disease called vegetitus. So I stay away from that stuff. Besides, green is a weird color. It's the same color as boogers. You shouldn't eat stuff that's green. That's the first rule of being a kid.

I was so depressed about 'Say Goodbye to Sugar' that I could hardly pay attention during social studies, math, reading, and science. I wasn't even excited when Miss Daisy announced that it was time to go to the computer lab to see Mrs. Yonkers. All I could think about was soda pop and junk food.

We had to walk a million hundred miles to the computer lab. It's in a trailer in the back of the parking lot, near the woods.

We walked up the ramp to the trailer.

We opened the door.

And you'll never believe what we saw in there.

3

Emily Is a Giant Hamster

There were a bunch of computers in the computer lab, of course! What did you *expect* to see in a computer lab? Man, are you dumb!

But there was something else in the computer lab, too. It was a wheel, like one of those wheels you see in a hamster cage. Except this one was six feet tall!

"Howdy, y'all!" Mrs. Yonkers said when we opened the door. She wasn't wearing her cheese head anymore. Instead, she was dressed in a jogging outfit and she had on a cowboy hat.

"Wow!" I said. "That's a big wheel!"

"Everything is bigger in Texas," said Mrs. Yonkers.

"What does it do?" asked Emily.

"It generates electricity. When I run inside the wheel, it powers the computer."

"Why not just plug the computer into the wall socket?" asked Neil the nude kid.

"This saves energy," Mrs. Yonkers

explained. "You burn less oil, and you have lower electric bills. Plus, I get exercise. It's a win-win!"

"It's cool!" we all agreed.

Mrs. Yonkers told us that she likes to use technology to solve problems. She even started her own computer company called NERD—New Electronic Research Development.

Mrs. Yonkers showed us a virtual reality helmet, night vision goggles, and some other cool stuff she invented.

"And here is a founding member of the company," she said as she pulled a big turtle out of a cage. "This is my friend Speedy."

"He's adorable!" said Andrea, who never misses the chance to brownnose a grown-up.

"What's that thing on his back?" asked Ryan.

"It's a tiny camera," said Mrs. Yonkers. "I call it Turtle Cam. While Speedy moves around the room, we'll be able to follow

his progress on my website."

"Can we see how it works?" asked Michael.

"I'm still ironing out the bugs," said Mrs. Yonkers.

"Please? Please? Please? Please?" everybody begged.

If you want anything from a grown-up, all you have to do is say "Please" until they can't stand it anymore. That's the first rule of being a kid.

"Well . . . okay," Mrs. Yonkers said, putting Speedy on the floor. "Who wants to run on the wheel to turn on the computer?"

"Me! Me! Me! Me!" everybody yelled.

Mrs. Yonkers did eenie meenie miney

moe. The last moe was Emily, the lucky stiff.

Emily climbed inside the wheel and started running. The wheel turned around, but the computer didn't turn on because Emily runs about as fast as Speedy the turtle.

"Faster, Emily! Faster!" we all yelled.

The computer screen started to flicker on when Emily ran faster. Speedy was walking around the room, and we could see a picture of what he was looking at. Turtle Cam was cool.

"Faster!" we all yelled. "Faster!"

Emily was running as hard as she could. The wheel was spinning really fast now and making a lot of noise. Speedy walked around to the front of the wheel. And that's when the weirdest thing in the history of the world happened.

The nuts and bolts that were holding the wheel to its frame must have gotten loose somehow. The wheel started rolling away!

It was heading for the wall!

Emily was still inside, and she was upside down!

"Watch out!" we all yelled.

Speedy barely got out of the way before the wheel crashed into the wall. We all rushed over there. Emily staggered out of the wheel, all dizzy, and fell down. She was on the floor, freaking out. It was hilarious.

"What happened?" Andrea asked Mrs. Yonkers.

"I guess the computer crashed," she replied.

Emily was shaken up pretty good, but it looked like she was going to be okay.

"Hey, where's Speedy?" asked Ryan.

We looked all around the computer lab. No Speedy.

"He's gone!" cried Mrs. Yonkers.

Sharpening Pencils Can Be Dangerous

Mrs. Yonkers wasn't too worried about Speedy the turtle. She said he runs away all the time. But thanks to Turtle Cam, she can usually find him. She turned on another computer, one that was plugged into the wall socket this time.

"There he is!" we shouted when Mrs.

Yonkers clicked on Turtle Cam.

"How did that rascal get outside?" she said. We all watched the screen closely. Speedy was heading toward some cars in the parking lot.

"Maybe he climbed out the window," Neil the nude kid guessed.

We saw some bushes on the computer screen, and then the screen got darker. All we could see were leaves and sticks.

"Speedy went into the woods!" I said.

"He'll be lost forever!" said Michael.

"We've got to do something!" shouted Emily, and she went running out of the room.

Emily is weird.

"Don't worry," said Mrs. Yonkers. "I'm sure Speedy will come back. In the meantime, would you like to see my latest top secret invention?"

"Yeah!" we all shouted.

Mrs. Yonkers took a small box out of her desk drawer.

"Is that a remote control?" I asked.

"Yes!" she said. "I'm a remote control *freak*! At home I use a remote control to open my

garage, turn on the TV and microwave, and even start my car. But this remote control is different. It's a *remote control* remote control!"

"What's a remote control remote control?" asked Ryan.

"It's a remote control you use when you don't feel like getting off the couch to pick up your regular remote control," said Mrs. Yonkers. "You just press a button on the remote control remote control, and then you can control your remote control."

"That's cool!" we all agreed. Mrs. Yonkers is a genius. She should get the No Bell Prize. That's a prize they give to people who don't have bells.

"You should invent a *remote control* remote control remote control," suggested Michael.

"That would be silly," Mrs. Yonkers said. She took another box out of her desk drawer. "But check this out. It's the world's first remote control pencil sharpener!"

"Wow!" we all said.

"How does it work?" I asked.

"You put your pencil in this little hole, and you can go as far as fifty feet away to turn it on," Mrs. Yonkers said. "Then you go back and get your pencil—all sharpened and ready to use."

"That's cool!" I said.

"Why would anybody want to do that?" asked Andrea. "Isn't it easier just to stay right there at the pencil sharpener?"

"It's cooler to sharpen pencils by remote control," I told Andrea. Doing *anything* by remote control is cool, if you ask me.

"Also, this is the first pencil sharpener that gives you a workout," Mrs. Yonkers explained. "I like to jog around the room while my pencil is being sharpened. It's a win-win!"

"Can we try it out?" asked Neil the nude kid.

"Well, I'm still ironing out the bugs," Mrs. Yonkers said.

"Please? Please? Please? Please?"

"Well . . . okay."

Mrs. Yonkers stuck a pencil into the sharpener. Then she picked up her remote control and led us over to the other end of the computer lab.

"Now watch this," she said, and she pushed a button on the remote. The pencil sharpener started making noises. We all clapped our hands. And then . . .

BAM!

There was a huge explosion! Pieces of pencil and pencil sharpener went flying all over the computer lab!

"Duck!" I shouted.

We all stopped, dropped, and rolled like

we do during a fire drill.

When we got up off the floor, there was smoke pouring out of what was left of the pencil sharpener. It was cool!

I thought Mrs. Yonkers was going to be upset that her remote control pencil sharpener had exploded into a million hundred pieces. But she didn't seem to mind at all.

"Lucky I used the remote control," she said. "We were out of harm's way, and nobody got hurt. Imagine how many kids would have been injured if we had used a *regular* pencil sharpener and it exploded. Remote control pencil sharpeners are much safer."

Mrs. Yonkers is bonkers!

Sugar
Shock

After dismissal, me and Michael and Ryan searched the woods behind the school for Speedy the turtle. We couldn't find him anywhere. I guess he ran away.

We were sad. But we were even sadder the next morning when we got to school. Two big guys wearing overalls were

wheeling the soda pop and candy machines out of the vomitorium, where wc cat lunch.

"Say good-bye to sugar!" cried Mrs. Cooney, who is beautiful. "From now on, there will only be healthy food at Ella Mentry School."

"NO!" I yelled, hugging the candy machine. "Don't take it away!"

Mrs. Cooney told me I was being silly. She said that after I stopped eating junk food, I wouldn't even miss it.

"Can I just say my good-byes to the soda and candy machines one last time?" I begged.

"Well, I suppose so," said Mrs. Cooney.

I got down on my knees in front of the machines. No more Good & Plenty. No more Almond Joy. No more Jujyfruits or M&M's or Starburst or Laffy Taffy. No more Sprite or Sierra Mist or Mountain Dew. No more junk food! How would we survive?

I thought I was gonna die. Tears started welling up in my eyes.

Michael suggested we have a moment of silence in honor of junk food. I thought that was a great idea. All the guys gathered around the machines.

During the moment of silence, I thought about all the good times we had eating candy and drinking soda pop. I even made up a poem for the occasion. I put my hand over my heart and recited it:

"I pledge allegiance
to the cans
of soda and bags of chips.
And to the yumminess
for which they stand,
two machines

in the vomitorium
with trans fats
and high fructose corn syrup
for all."

Some other kids joined us and watched as the guys in overalls loaded up the machines and wheeled them out of the vomitorium. We were all sniffling.

That's when Andrea and her annoying girly friends came over.

"What's the big deal?" she asked. "I like to eat healthy snacks like carrot sticks and fresh fruit. Kids should have a balanced diet."

I wish her diet would get unbalanced

and fall on her head.

All I could think about that morning was junk food. While Miss Daisy was telling the class about precipitation (which is just some fancy grown-up word for rain and snow), I was searching through my desk for something to eat. A Tootsie Roll Pop. A Smartie. A Froot Loops. A tic tac. ANYTHING.

"I need sugar!" I whispered to Ryan. "I'm dying!"

Finally, in my back pocket, I found something. An old LifeSaver! It was covered with so much lint that I couldn't even tell what flavor it was. But I ate it anyway. Sometimes, in a survival situation, a man's gotta do what a man's gotta do.

I guess that's why they call LifeSavers lifesavers. Because that LifeSaver *was* a lifesaver!

Computers Can't Tell Jokes

We were still depressed about the junk food shortage when we got to computer class that afternoon. When we walked into the lab, Mrs. Yonkers was sitting on top of her desk, and her computer was on her chair. That was weird. You're supposed to sit on your *chair* with the computer on your *desk*.

It was also weird that Mrs. Yonkers had no shoes on. She was typing with her toes.

"Why are you typing with your toes, Mrs. Yonkers?" asked Emily.

"I have *so* much work to do," she told us. "When I type with my feet, it leaves my hands free to do something else. So I get twice as much work done. It's a win-win!"

"What are you typing, Mrs. Yonkers?" asked Andrea.

"E-mails," she replied.

"To who?" asked Ryan.

"To myself," Mrs. Yonkers said. "I love getting e-mail."

It seemed to me that Mrs. Yonkers would get *twice* as much work done if she didn't spend half her time writing e-mails to herself. Why are grown-ups so weird?

"Did you find Speedy the turtle?" asked Neil the nude kid.

"Not yet," said Mrs. Yonkers. "I've been

too busy thinking about Mr. Klutz's problem."

"What problem?" asked Emily.

"The other day he said it was too bad there isn't a computer program that makes up jokes," Mrs. Yonkers said. "So I started working on one. It's called Giggle."

"Oooh, can we try it?" I asked. *"Please? Please? Please? Please?"*

"Well . . . okay."

Mrs. Yonkers pulled a sheet off a computer in the corner and turned it on. The screen showed the word GIGGLE with an empty box under it. Mrs. Yonkers told us that if you type any word in the box, Giggle will make up a joke about that word.

"Skateboarding!" I shouted.

"Flowers!" Andrea shouted.

"Boogers!" Michael shouted.

We called out all kinds of suggestions until Neil the nude kid said, "Pig!" We all agreed it would be cool to read jokes about pigs.

Mrs. Yonkers typed PIG in the box and hit the ENTER kcy. The computer thought about it for a few seconds, and then it showed us a pig joke:

Q: WHY DO PIGS GO OINK?
A: BECAUSE FIREMEN BANANA
STOMACH PITCHFORK!

"I don't get it," said Andrea.

"That doesn't make any sense," said Emily.

"Computers aren't very good at understanding language," said Mrs. Yonkers. "I'm still ironing out some of the bugs."

I didn't get the joke either, but I started laughing my head off anyway. If Andrea doesn't think something is funny, it must be.

"Firemen banana stomach pitchfork!" I howled. "That's hilarious!"

Ryan and Michael and Neil the nude kid joined in too. Soon the whole class was cracking up, except Andrea and Emily.

"You're a bunch of dumbheads," Andrea said.

I must admit, that pig joke was actually pretty lame. But it was just as funny as Mr. Klutz's jokes, if you ask me.

Busted!

Life without candy and soda pop is a horrible, meaningless existence. Now that the junk food machines were gone from the vomitorium, I was left with no choice. It was time to resort to extreme measures.

I decided to sneak in junk food from home.

The next morning I stuffed a bag of Cracker Jacks into my backpack. I jammed some Reese's Peanut Butter Cups in my pencil case. I put some popcorn in my pants pockets. I had a Charleston Chew in my shoe and gummi bears in my underwear!

"I'm a walking candy store," I whispered to Michael and Ryan as we went through the front doors of school.

BEEP! BEEP! BEEP!

Bells started ringing and sirens started blaring.

"JUNK FOOD ALERT!" announced this computery voice. "JUNK FOOD ALERT!"

Suddenly some guy in a police uniform jumped out from behind the door. He had a gun, handcuffs, and one of those clubs they use to beat up the bad guys on TV.

"Freeze, dirtbag!" he yelled.

"Huh?" I asked. "Who are you?"

"My name is Officer Spence!" he said, pulling my hands behind my back. "I'm the new security guard here. Are you hiding any junk food on your person, young man?"

"You are so busted, A.J.," said Ryan.

I emptied my pockets for Officer Spence. I handed over the Reese's Peanut

Butter Cups, the popcorn, the gummi bears, the Cracker Jacks, and the Charleston Chews, too.

"Step away from the junk food," ordered Officer Spence, "and nobody gets hurt."

By that time a crowd of kids had gathered around to see what all the excitement was about.

"Is Arlo going to jail?" Andrea asked with a huge grin on her face.

"I'm going to let you off with a warning this time, young man," Officer Spence told me. "But don't bring any more junk food to school. That is, if you know what's good for you."

"Yes sir," I said meekly.

Ryan and Michael were laughing their heads off like it was the funniest thing in the history of the world. But it wasn't funny to *me*. I thought about running away to Antarctica to live with the penguins, but it would probably be even harder to get junk food there.

"I have to run some tests on this evidence to make sure it's not poisoned," Officer Spence said as he bit into one of my Reese's Peanut Butter Cups. "You can't be too careful, you know."

"Hey, that's *my* candy!" I complained.

"There might be a bomb in these Cracker Jacks," Officer Spence said, ripping open the bag. "I'd better test them."

He stuffed a fistful of Cracker Jacks

into his mouth.

"This batch is clean," he said. "Lucky I was here to make sure."

Officer Spence makes no sense!

But there was something else I still didn't understand. What the heck was it that started beeping when I went through the front door?

That's when Mr. Klutz came running down the hall. He was all excited.

"The new infrared heat-sensing digital junk food detector *works!*" he said. "Mrs. Yonkers is a genius!"

What?! This was one of Mrs. Yonkers's inventions? It was a horrible, terrible, mean invention, if you ask me.

I was really mad at Mrs. Yonkers.

Virtual Reality Day

I was so mad that I wouldn't even look at Mrs. Yonkers when we walked into the computer lab that afternoon.

"Is something wrong, A.J.?" she asked.

"Yes, something is wrong," I replied. "Your junk food detector is a horrible, terrible, mean invention!"

She took me outside the computer lab, and I told her how Officer Spence humiliated me in front of the whole school.

"He took away my junk food and ate it!" I complained. "I love junk food. I *need* junk food."

"Oh dear!" said Mrs. Yonkers. "This is terrible. I thought I was solving a problem for Mr. Klutz. I didn't realize I was making one for you."

Mrs. Yonkers was really nice about it. She said she would think of a way to make it up to me. When we went back into the computer lab, I wasn't so mad anymore.

"Today is Virtual Reality Day!" Mrs. Yonkers announced to the class.

She gave each of us a strange-looking helmet. When I put mine on, I couldn't see the computer lab anymore. Instead, I saw a big green field with a castle! I took a step forward, and it looked like I was walking *toward* the castle. It was freaky weird.

"Mrs. Yonkers!" announced Mrs. Patty, the school secretary, over the loudspeaker.

"Please
come to the office."

"Oh dear," Mrs. Yonkers
said. "I'll be right back."

She told us to be on our
best behavior while she was
gone. So as soon as she left the room, I
shook my butt at the class. But nobody
laughed because we all had our virtual
reality helmets on.

I went up to the virtual castle in front of me and started exploring it. I thought all the other kids were seeing the same thing I was, but everyone saw something different.

"I'm walking in a barren desert world," Ryan said.

"I'm on a busy street," Michael said.

"I'm in outer space," Andrea said.

We were all stumbling around the computer lab like zombies in a horror movie. Virtual reality is cool.

"Too bad we don't have laser guns," Neil the nude kid said.

"Yeah," I agreed. "Then we could shoot each other."

"Why do boys constantly think about shooting things?" asked Andrea. "Can't you have fun without hurting other people?"

"No," I told her.

Me and Andrea started a virtual argument, but we didn't have the chance to finish it because we were interrupted. You'll never believe who walked into the door at that very moment.

It was Emily! She walked right into the door!

"Owwwww!" she howled.

Emily was on the floor, freaking out. What a crybaby!

"I hit my head on the door!" she whined. "I think I have brain damage!"

"No, that happened a long time ago," I cracked. Some of the kids laughed.

Suddenly Mrs. Yonkers came running back into the computer lab.

"Oh dear!" she said. "What happened?"

"Dumbhead walked into the door," I explained.

Mrs. Yonkers sat down on the floor and held Emily's head in her arms. Then she did the weirdest thing in the history of the world. She started crying too!

"I'm so sorry!" she cried. "I'm still ironing out some

of the bugs in the virtual reality helmets. The pressure of this new job and my company is starting to get to me. I'm worried about Speedy, too. He's never been gone for so long."

"It's okay, Mrs. Yonkers," Emily said. "I'll be all right."

"It's just that I have so many ideas rumbling around in my head," Mrs. Yonkers told us. "There's so much I need to accomplish, and I have so little time to do it. Sometimes I wish I could clone myself."

I didn't feel bad for that crybaby Emily. She falls down for no reason every five minutes. But I *did* feel bad for Mrs. Yonkers. She was a nice lady, even if her inventions were weird.

The Truth About Mrs. Yonkers

The next day we were sitting around the vomitorium eating lunch when an announcement came over the loud-speaker.

"Mrs. Yonkers is absent today," said Mrs. Patty. "All computer classes are canceled."

Bummer in the summer!

At the next table, the girls were talking about silly stuff, like what dress they should wear to somebody's birthday party and how many rubber bands they should put in their hair. We boys had more important things to talk about.

"I can hang a spoon from my nose," Ryan said.

"No way," I said.

Ryan breathed on his spoon. Then he put the spoon on his nose and it hung there! It was the most amazing thing in the history of the world.

Ryan taught me and Michael and Neil the nude kid how to hang spoons from our noses. After that we had a spoon-hanging contest. Ryan won, because he was able to

hang four spoons from his face at the same time. He should be in the gifted and talented program like me.

I opened the lunch bag that my mom packed. Milk. A bag of peanuts. An apple. Carrot sticks.

Ugh! I hate healthy food. I can't believe we're supposed to eat fruits and vegetables. They grow out of the dirt! That's disgusting!

I looked over at the girls' table.

"Andrea," said Emily, "do you want to trade your stir-fried veggies and fruit kabobs for my tofu nuggets?"

"No thanks," Andrea replied. "I'm not hungry."

Andrea looked all sad, like her dog died or something.

"What's the matter with you?" I asked. "Did your dog die or something?"

"I'm worried about Mrs. Yonkers," Andrea said.

"What about her?" asked Michael.

"She's under so much pressure," Andrea said. "My mother is a psychologist. She says that when people are under a lot of pressure, they could have a nervous breakdown."

"Maybe Mrs. Yonkers isn't a computer teacher at all," I suggested. "Did you ever think of that?"

"What do you mean?" asked Emily.

"Well, maybe she's just *pretending* to be

a computer teacher."

"Yeah," said Ryan. "Maybe Mrs. Yonkers is an evil genius who kidnaps computer teachers and forces them to hack into government computer networks. Stuff like that happens all the time, you know."

"It does?" Emily asked.

"Stop trying to scare Emily," said Andrea.

"Sure it does," Michael said. "Maybe Mrs. Yonkers is planning to program

all the computers in the world to crash at the same time."

"Yeah," said Neil the nude kid, "and maybe she tied up our *real* computer teacher in the secret dungeon in the basement."

"I think they moved the secret dungeon up to the third floor," Ryan said.

"I'll bet Mrs. Yonkers took apart a laser printer, and she's going to torture our real computer teacher with laser beams," I added. "I saw that in a movie once."

"We've got to *do* something!" Emily shouted. Then she went running out of the vomitorium.

Emily is weird.

The Greatest Invention in the History of the World

The next morning Mr. Klutz came into our class with his bald head.

"Tomorrow Dr. Carbles is coming to visit our school," said Mr. Klutz. "He's the president of the Board of Education. He wants to see if we're making any progress with bringing our school into the 21st century. So I expect all of you to be on your very best behavior."

"We will!" we all said.

"Is our computer teacher tied up in the dungeon, being shot with laser beams?" Emily asked.

"Not that I know of," Mr. Klutz replied. "In fact, I think Mrs. Yonkers is in the computer lab, working on her lesson plans now."

We were all happy that Mrs. Yonkers was back at school. But when we saw her in the computer lab, she looked really tired. She told us she didn't get any sleep last night.

"I was thinking about you kids," she

told us, "and I think I came up with the solution to your problem."

She pulled a sheet off a computer in the corner. Attached to the computer was a box that looked sort of like a big microwave oven.

"What's that?" Michael asked.

"I call it the JFT," Mrs. Yonkers said. "Junk Food Transformer. Watch this."

She took a piece of broccoli out of a bag on her desk and put it in the Junk Food Transformer. Then she typed something on the computer keyboard. The microwave thing buzzed for a minute or so, and then a bell rang. Mrs. Yonkers opened the door. And you'll never

believe what was in there.

A York Peppermint Pattie!

"Wow!" we all shouted.

"What happened to the broccoli?" asked Andrea.

"The Junk Food Transformer turned it into a York Peppermint Pattie!" said Mrs. Yonkers. She unwrapped the Peppermint

Pattie and took a bite out of it.

"That's impossible!" Ryan said. "It's a trick!"

"You think so?" Mrs. Yonkers asked. "Well, watch *this*."

She took a handful of green beans—the most vile and disgusting food in the history of the world—and put it into the Junk Food Transformer. Then she typed something on the keyboard. The microwave thing started buzzing again. When the bell rang and Mrs. Yonkers opened the door, do you know what was inside?

Three Hershey's bars!

"Wow!" we all shouted.

Mrs. Yonkers peeled off a wrapper and

gave each of us a piece.

"It tastes just like chocolate!" marveled Michael.

"It *is* chocolate," said Mrs. Yonkers, "yet it has all the vitamins and nutrients of green beans! The Junk Food Transformer turns health food into healthy *junk* food."

"It's amazing!" said Andrea.

"You should get the No Bell Prize," I told Mrs. Yonkers.

"Say, can the Junk Food Transformer turn junk food into health food?" asked Ryan.

"Why would anybody want to do that?" I asked.

Ryan is weird.

Mrs. Yonkers said it was okay for us to go back to our classroom and get our healthy lunches from our cubbies. I never ran so fast in my whole life. When we got back to the computer lab, Mrs. Yonkers had a grocery bag filled with fruits and vegetables on her desk. We spent the rest of class turning all the health food into junk food.

It was the greatest day of my life. We made Milk Duds and Sugar Daddys. AirHeads and WarHeads. Ring Pops and Push Pops and Blow Pops and Pop Rocks. We ended up with so much candy, gum, and lollipops that it looked like Halloween. There was no way we could eat it all.

When the bell rang and it was time to go, we stashed a bunch of candy in Mrs. Yonkers's closet.

"This is the greatest invention in the history of the world!" I told Mrs. Yonkers.

"Shhhhh," she said. "Don't tell anybody yet. It will be our little secret!"

Send in the Clones

Keeping secrets is *hard*. I wanted to tell my parents about the Junk Food Transformer. I wanted to tell my friend Billy who lives around the corner. I wanted to tell *somebody*.

But I didn't. My lips were sealed. (But not with glue or anything. That would be weird.)

The next morning Mrs. Patty made an announcement over the loudspeaker.

"Mrs. Yonkers is absent today, but please go to the computer lab at your regularly scheduled time."

That was weird. If Mrs. Yonkers was absent, who would be our computer teacher? All day long we wondered. Finally, it was time for computer class.

We rushed down the hall.

We opened the door of the computer lab.

And you'll never believe in a million hundred years who was standing there.

It was a *robot*!

"SIT DOWN," the robot commanded in a computery voice. "PAY ATTENTION."

SIT DOWN

The robot looked a lot like Mrs. Yonkers. It even wore a NERDS R COOL T-shirt and a fake cheese head.

"MRS. YONKERS IS NOT FEELING WELL," the robot said. "I AM MRS. ROBO-YONKERS. I WILL BE YOUR TEACHER TODAY."

Wow! Mrs. Yonkers built her own robot substitute teacher! Cool! We used to have a sub named Ms. Todd. But then she tried to murder Miss Daisy and take her job. Ms. Todd was odd.

"Remember Mrs. Yonkers told us that she had so much work, she wished she could clone herself?" Andrea said as we sat down. "Well, I guess she figured out how to do it."

Clones are cool. My friend Billy who lives around the corner told me that scientists have cloned sheep, cats, and cows. But nobody ever cloned a person before.

"STOP TALKING," said Mrs. Robo-Yonkers. "FOLD YOUR FEET. KEEP YOUR HANDS ON THE FLOOR."

She sounded almost like a real teacher!

"Mrs. Robo-Yonkers," I said. "I have a

question."

"STATE YOUR QUESTION," said Mrs. Robo-Yonkers.

"Firemen banana stomach pitchfork?" I asked.

"I DO NOT UNDERSTAND THE QUESTION," said Mrs. Robo-Yonkers. "PLEASE REPEAT THE QUESTION."

"Football my orange telephone?" I asked.

"DOES NOT COMPUTE," said Mrs. Robo-Yonkers. "PLEASE REPEAT."

"Watermelon lawn chair atomic bicycle?" I asked.

"What are you doing, Arlo?" asked Andrea.

"Computers aren't very good at understanding language," I said. "I'm yanking her chain. That's what you're supposed to do with substitute teachers. It's the first rule of being a kid."

"I DO NOT UNDERSTAND," said Mrs. Robo-Yonkers.

"Monster my upside down moon machine?" I asked.

"Stop it, Arlo!" Andrea said. "You're going to get us in trouble!"

But it was too late. We were already in trouble. Mrs. Robo-Yonkers started shaking and twitching.

"SYSTEM ERROR! SYSTEM ERROR! SYSTEM ERROR!" she droned.

Smoke was coming out of her head,

and sparks were shooting out of her neck. She started turning around in circles and bumping into desks.

"I think she blew a circuit!" said Michael.

Mrs. Robo-Yonkers was rolling crazily around the computer lab, crashing into everything in her path. Kids were diving out of the way.

"Run for your lives!" shouted Neil the nude kid.

"I'll get Mr. Klutz!" yelled Andrea as she ran out of the lab.

Mrs. Robo-Yonkers was bouncing around the computer lab like a pinball. She was out of control. Finally, Mr. Klutz came running in.

"What's wrong?" he yelled.

"Mrs. Robo-Yonkers has gone berserk!" I told him.

"Leave it to me," Mr. Klutz said. "I used to work with computers in my younger days. Where does Mrs. Yonkers keep the robot's remote control?"

"In a remote location," I said.

"SYSTEM ERROR! SYSTEM ERROR! SYSTEM ERROR!"

As Mrs. Robo-Yonkers spun around in circles, one of her arms hit Emily before she could duck out of the way.

"Owwww! My head!" Emily was on the floor, freaking out as usual.

"Call Mrs. Cooney!" shouted Mr. Klutz. "Tell her to bring her first-aid kit!"

Mrs. Robo-Yonkers was running around

the computer lab. Mr. Klutz was running around the computer lab. All of us kids were running around the computer lab. It was a lot like that scene in the movie *King Kong* when Kong broke his chains and went running around the streets of New York. Everybody was going crazy.

And you'll never believe who showed up at that very moment.

It was Dr. Carbles, the president of the Board of Education! Oh, snap!

"Klutz!" Dr. Carbles shouted. "What's the meaning of this?"

"Nothing to worry about, sir," Mr. Klutz said, as Mrs. Robo-Yonkers crashed into the whiteboard.

"Why is it that every time I visit this

school, the students are running around like lunatics?" demanded Dr. Carbles. "These kids are obviously hopped up on junk food!"

"Oh no, sir!" said Mr. Klutz. "We got rid of all the junk food. We even put in a junk food detector at the front door."

At that very moment, Mrs. Robo-Yonkers rammed into the closet where we hid all the candy the day before. Twinkies and Twix and Jolly Ranchers and Skittles and Chuckles went flying all over the place.

"Klutz!" yelled Dr. Carbles. "What's the meaning of this? I thought you got rid of all the junk food."

"We did!" Mr. Klutz said. "Somebody get Mrs. Yonkers on the phone!"

That's when Mrs. Cooney (who is beautiful) came running in with her first-aid kit. She took out her cell phone and started dialing frantically. Mrs. Robo-Yonkers was chasing Dr. Carbles around the computer lab. It was just like in that King Kong movie.

Mrs. Robo-Yonkers was bonkers!

One Way to Handle a Sub

"Everyone stay calm!" yelled the beautiful Mrs. Cooney. "Mrs. Yonkers is on her way over. She'll know what to do."

Mrs. Cooney put a bag of ice on Emily's head, while Mrs. Robo-Yonkers chased Dr. Carbles around the computer lab. Finally Mrs. Yonkers arrived with her cheese head.

"What's the big emergency?" she asked.

"Your robot clone is crazy!" yelled Mr. Klutz.

"Help!" yelled Dr. Carbles. "She's trying to kill me!"

"Oh dear," said Mrs. Yonkers. "I guess I still have to work out some of the bugs."

"How do we stop her?" cried Mrs. Cooney.

"There's only one thing to do," Mrs. Yonkers said as she pulled a remote control out of her pocket. "I must destroy Mrs. Robo-Yonkers. Everybody stand back."

Mrs. Robo-Yonkers had Dr. Carbles pinned against the whiteboard. We all hid our eyes. I waited for the sound of the explosion.

But nothing hap-
pened. The only sound
I heard was Mrs. Yonkers
crying.

"I can't do it," Mrs.
Yonkers sobbed as she
handed the remote control
to Mrs. Cooney. "Here, *you*
do it. Push the button marked
SELF-DESTRUCT."

Dr. Carbles crawled between Mrs.
Robo-Yonkers's legs and ran away. Mrs.
Cooney pushed the button.

One second . . .

Two seconds . . .

Three seconds . . .

"DUCK!" I shouted.

BAM! There was a big explosion. Pieces of Mrs. Robo-Yonkers went flying everywhere. Her head landed on top of the flagpole in the corner of the computer lab.

"I'll be back," the head said. And then it fell into the garbage can.

It was a real Kodak moment. You should have been there! And we got to see it live and in person.

When it was all over, Mrs. Yonkers was sitting on the floor, crying.

"Boo hoo," she cried. "I created Mrs. Robo-Yonkers with my bare hands. I'm sorry. I didn't mean for all this to happen."

We told Mrs. Yonkers it wasn't *her* fault that her clone went crazy and attacked

I'll Be Back! the president of the Board of Education. And that's when Little Miss Big Mouth had to open her trap.

"It's all Arlo's fault," said Andrea. "If he hadn't said all those weird sentences to Mrs. Robo-Yonkers, none of this would have happened. You killed her, Arlo!"

"No, I didn't kill her," I said as I pointed at Mrs. Cooney. "Twas beauty that killed the beast."

13

The Moral of the Story

We were all pretty bummed that Mrs. Robo-Yonkers exploded. Especially Mrs. Yonkers. All of us kids gathered around to hug her. And that's when the most amazing thing in the history of the world happened. Somebody walked into the computer lab, and you'll never believe in a million hundred years who it was.

I'm not going to tell you.

Okay, okay. I'll tell you.

It was Speedy the turtle!

"Speedy!" yelled Mrs. Yonkers. "You came back!"

She picked up Speedy and hugged him and kissed his shell. We were all so happy to see him, no one seemed to care anymore that Mrs. Robo-Yonkers exploded. If you ask me, Mrs. Yonkers loved Speedy

more than she loved Mrs. Robo-Yonkers anyway.

Well, the moral of the story is . . . that there *is* no moral of the story. Who decided that stories have to have morals anyway? Sometimes weird stuff just happens for no good reason. Especially at *my* weird school.

Maybe Mrs. Yonkers will be able to build a new robot clone. Maybe she'll make a million dollars from the Junk Food Transformer. Or maybe she'll make a computer that you plug into your head so we don't have to go to school anymore. Maybe she'll stop writing e-mails to herself. Maybe Emily will stop falling down and Andrea will stop being so annoying. Maybe I'll find a way to live in a world without junk food. Maybe we'll travel through time to the 21st century.

But it won't be easy!

Check out the My Weird School series!

#1: Miss Daisy Is Crazy!

The first book in the hilarious series stars A.J., a second grader who hates school—and can't believe his teacher hates it too!

#2: Mr. Klutz Is Nuts!

A.J. can't believe his crazy principal wants to climb to the top of the flagpole!

#3: Mrs. Roopy Is Loopy!

The new librarian thinks she's George Washington one day and Little Bo Peep the next!

#4: Ms. Hannah Is Bananas!

The art teacher wears clothes made from pot holders. Worse than that, she's trying to make A.J. be partners with yucky Andrea!

#5: Miss Small Is off the Wall!

The gym teacher is teaching A.J.'s class to juggle scarves, balance feathers, and do everything *but* play sports!

#6: Mr. Hynde Is Out of His Mind!

The music teacher plays bongo drums on the principal's bald head! But does he have what it takes to be a real rock-and-roll star?

#7: Mrs. Cooney Is Loony!

The school nurse is everybody's favorite—but is she hiding a secret identity?

#8: Ms. LaGrange Is Strange!

The new lunch lady talks funny—and why is she writing secret messages in the mashed potatoes?

#9: Miss Lazar Is Bizarre!

What kind of grown-up *likes* cleaning throw-up? Miss Lazar is the weirdest custodian in the world!

#10: Mr. Docker Is off His Rocker!

The science teacher alarms and amuses A.J.'s class with his wacky experiments and nutty inventions.

#11: Mrs. Kormel Is Not Normal!

A.J.'s school bus gets a flat tire, then becomes hopelessly lost at the hands of the wacky bus driver.

#12: Ms. Todd Is Odd!

Ms. Todd is subbing, and A.J. and his friends are sure she kidnapped Miss Daisy so she could take over her job.

#13: Mrs. Patty Is Batty!

A little bit of spookiness and a lot of humor add up to the best trick-or-treating adventure ever!

#14: Miss Holly Is Too Jolly!

When Miss Holly decks the hall with mistletoe, A.J. knows to watch out. Mistletoe means kissletoe, the worst tradition in the history of the world!

#15: Mr. Macky Is Wacky!

Mr. Macky expects A.J. and his friends to read stuff about the presidents…and even dress up like them! He's taking Presidents' Day way too far!

#16: Ms. Coco Is Loco!

It's Poetry Month and the whole school is poetry crazy, thanks to Ms. Coco. She talks in rhyme! She thinks boys should have feelings! Is she crazy?

#17: Miss Suki Is Kooky!

Miss Suki is a famous author who writes about endangered animals. But when her pet raptor gets loose during a school visit, it's the kids who are endangered!

Also look for
#19: Dr. Carbles Is Losing His Marbles!

Dr. Carbles, the president of the board of education, is fed up with Mr. Klutz and wants to fire him. Will A.J. and his friends be able to save their principal's job?

HarperTrophy®
An Imprint of HarperCollinsPublishers

www.harpercollinschildrens.com   **www.dangutman.com**